CW01468152

EBB'S DAL

A not so short story for grown up children

THE SEED

Long, long ago in the dim and distant beginnings, before people had thought of time and age and the gods and goddesses were still their neighbours; in a beautiful soft green land, far beyond the misty mountains of dawn and past the source of the river of antiquity, there lived a farmer and his name was Sky.

Since the first stirrings of things Sky had farmed the land with his wife whom he called Laughter but whose real name was Meadow. Though they had borne no children of their own, the land and the living things of the land had been children to them and they had always been content. Thus they had journeyed together through a world cycle of service. Their love was as deep as the roots of the earth and as brilliant as the stars and the heavens smiled upon their days.

Then one day Laughter took to her sick bed. She fought there long and hard, through fire and through ice. Sky tended her and stayed at her side but the storm raged strong and she grew weak and frail. Finally, one long, wet, fearful winter's night the lightening came to take her on a new journey. Sky woke the next morning to find her still and cold and his grief was as broad as the wings of creation.

At the centre of their farm, there was a small hill with a beautiful view of the surrounding valley. Sky decided that this would be a fitting place for his beloved wife to take her long sleep, where she could watch over the farm that she had devoted her life to and where her spirit could protect all those who would farm there after her. He carried her there and laid her body in the ground.

With words of love and blessing, but not of parting, he covered her in a warm blanket or the rich dark earth that they had served together, and been served by, and he began to weep. So deep and so long was his loss that his weeping became a storm to equal the fever that had taken her from him and his spirit took wings to guide her to the worlds beyond. There by her graveside he sat for several days and nights and an unquenchable river of tears flowed from his unseeing eyes.

After what felt like an eternity of darkness the first waves of his grief slackened and he drew breath and sat up straight... again he drew breath and wiped his eyes. There before him, where his tears had fallen onto the grave and moistened the earth, a small plant had sprouted out. This sight was spring to his winter. He did not recognise the plant but it's leaves were bright innocence and it radiated such a strength in it's newly-found joy of life that for a moment the sun shone through the clouds of his loss in rays of orange comfort. He realised now that he was very hungry and dry so he stood up and returned home.

Over the following years Sky took great care of this plant. He built a small fence around it to protect it from grazing animals. He watered it when the seasons were dry and shaded it when the sun was too hot. He fed it with rich soils and tender care and he covered it when the winters were harsh. He named the plant after his wife and when the evenings were warm he would sit on the hill surveying the farm and talk to this young plant as if it were his close friend and confidante. So, from the grave of his lost love this new plant of hope grew strong and healthy until, before long, it was a small tree... and this, it is said, is how the first Apple tree came into being.

When the tree reached maturity, it began to produce fruit. In fact it began to produce vast quantities of fruit. Huge crops of the sweetest, most heavenly tasting apples; which sky harvested and, those that he could not eat or give away, he sold as part of his farm produce. They were received eagerly by all those who tasted them and they became famed throughout the land for their fresh sweetness and full-some flavour. As the apple tree grew it produced so much fruit that harvesting, storing and distributing them occupied most of Sky's time.

So the tree and its abundance of fruits were a balm to this farmer's loss and the greatest joy of his twilight years.

THE FRUIT

The tree grew strong and healthy and it had a vibrancy and life that shone. For this was no ordinary tree. It was a tree born of magical origins, drawn into being by the forces of love and loss, of despair and hope; It's very body a living link between Sky and Meadow. For the rest of Sky's life, the tree reminded him of Laughter, his beloved wife who awaited him in the worlds to come. With its harvest, it continued to pour forth the fruits of their love. And it continued to do so long after Sky's memory had become softened into the mists of legend.

Beneath the apple tree's bounty farmers came and went. Generations and peoples passed before it like ripples on the surface of a wind blown shore. The world turned and the tree lived on, for a life born of magic and love does not fade as easily a one born of the soil. Through years beyond memory and seasons beyond count men harvested fruit from the tree whose life-span was measured in ages, not winters. Until it simply became something that had always been. Above its branches the moon waxed and waned more times than the heartbeats of a long and healthy life and the tree grew heavy under the weight of it's own giving. The story of the creation of the tree passed into local myth and the people of that land revered it like a sacred shrine.

Many, many moons later, when the tree was unknowably ancient, those people had become more like the people of today- except that they had not yet begun to think that they understood how the universe worked and therefore strange things still happened more easily.

At this time, the valley in which the tree grew was farmed by a man called Ebb. Like many of the people of that area he claimed to be a direct descendant of Sky but whether that was meant literally or figuratively in those days it is hard to tell.

Like Sky, Ebb was a widower but, unlike Sky, he was not alone. He had four loving daughters who were filled with their mother's joy of living and were the light in his life and his reason for being. Now a very unusual situation had arisen in Ebb's household. For, although his four daughters were not at-all of the same age, it just so happened that, during the course of this year, each of them had fallen in love and then announced that they would marry the following spring. Naturally this brought Ebb great joy, for he was not a young man and was happy that his daughters should have new families to care for them when he no longer could. But it also brought him a small worry.

You see Ebb was not a poor man, but nor was he a rich man. As a family they had farmed the land and lived happily but simply. He had put some small savings aside expecting (and perhaps hoping) that a dowry may be needed one day soon… but to suddenly have four weddings in the same year.! This was more than he had hoped for and certainly more than he had planned for. What could he offer his daughters to give them a good start in their new lives? He did not know. Yet his daughters meant everything to him and he wanted to be able to give them gifts that would reflect the measure of his love. This was a matter to which he would give the most careful attention.

One warm evening early in the fall he was walking home late across the farm and this problem was laying heavily upon his mind. He decided to walk up to the old apple tree on the hill and sit for a while in thought. It was a peaceful spot which he often came to when he needed to make a decision or solve a problem, as had members of his family for many generations. There was a special quality to this place. The tree was like on old family friend and trusted advisor. The whole hill had an air of the sacred.

Ebb sat for a long time that evening, thinking of how long his fore-fathers had lived on this land, how different their lives had been and how many difficult situations they must have overcome. He tried to think of things that he could make as gifts for his daughters, or something that he could do for them that would rightly express his joy at their weddings and the depth of his love. He sat with his back to the ancient apple tree and wondered how many droughts and storms and long, cold winters it had survived here on this hill. He gave thanks to the tree for the bounteous harvest of apples that it still produced yearly and that were still relished by all who tasted them.

Some way into the night he came to as if from a deep sleep, or a light sleep, he could not tell. The night was beginning to turn cold. The sky was clear and the stars bright. Though he was no nearer a solution to his problem, as far as he could tell, somehow he felt lighter. He thanked the tree for it's company and returned home.

Soon the business of the harvest distracted his mind from the matter of the wedding gifts and it was not till late in the year that he climbed up the hill again to visit the old apple tree. This time however he was not alone and he did not intend to sit and contemplate. The crop of apples on the tree was ripe for the picking and he was here with his daughters to harvest them.

An unusual thing happened while they were harvesting the apples that year. They began, as always, by collecting the apples on the lower branches that could be reached from the ground, and this tree was so large and so bountiful that these alone filled several large boxes. Once this was done ladders were used to reach the higher branches. Whoever was smallest and lightest would collect the fruit from the topmost and outermost branches so as to cause least harm to the old tree. These were passed down chain-style to the people on the ground for packing.

So it was that late one afternoon Ebb's youngest and lightest daughter Issy (Isabel) was balanced on the end of a long ladder collecting the last fruit from the topmost branches. She knew well that when an apple is perfectly ripe it takes only the gentlest of touches to part it from the tree. Those that are not quite ripe are harvested with a swift tug and they ripen latter in storage. She had spotted what looked like a particularly plump and ripe fruit out on the end of one of the last branches and was surprised therefore, when she had finally worked her way round to it, that it did not come of with ease. She tried again more firmly and still it did not yield. She called with amusement for the others to watch and, carefully balanced, she pulled on the fruit with all her might. She pulled and strained until the whole limb of the tree arched towards her and still the fruit remained firmly connected to the tree. She had the impression that a thread of iron was running from the fruit through the branch and trunk and down into the roots of the tree and it didn't seem to want to let this one go.

This was most unusual but the day was late and they had yet to carry the harvest home so she gave a shrug of confused resignation and moved on to clear the remaining few branches. As they were leaving that evening she glanced back at the tree where the unpick-able apple was clearly visible hanging proudly on the end of that high branch.

Winter was cold that year and set in early. Ebb and his daughters soon settled into their winter routines. The stocks of food and wood were high and they rarely ventured far from the house. So nobody noticed when the first frost touched that plump unpick-able apple, still clinging to the top-most limb of the apple tree up on the hill, that it turned a crisp golden brown. The winters grip slowly tightened. The land hardened and the colour of the apple deepened to a dark woody brown, the colour of the trunk of the tree. A passer-by would not have recognised it as an apple at all but would have thought it to be a rounded woody growth on the branch.

But nobody passed by. Drifts of snow covered the valley. Filling in the cracks, smoothing off the corners and softening everything with a pristine monochrome icing of white. Trips out were taken only when necessary and these were taken quietly and well wrapped up.

Most people stayed at home and stoked their fires. Now there was plenty of time for contemplation and planning. Ebb's mind wandered regularly to the spring and to the four weddings that would happen at the same time. He had made at least one decision on the matter.

Since he was a farmer and his life was devoted to providing food for people then, on the occasion of his daughter's weddings, he would provide the largest and most lavish feast that anybody from the whole region could ever remember seeing. A feast so fulsome and abundant that when the guests had eaten their fill so much food should remain that each could take home enough to feed their families for a month to come. His daughters should leave with such cart-loads of supplies that they need not worry about what they should eat for a whole year or more.

This idea gave him joy and had gone some way to settling his mind but he in no way thought that a cart load of food, however bountiful and rare, was a good enough dowry for one of his daughters. He dearly wanted to give them so much more. He wished for them to leave for their new homes with a gift from him that was of real and lasting value.

Yet, despite the strength of this desire he felt an odd sense of inner contentment and trust. Since the evening spent sitting under the old apple tree on the hill this problem had weighed less heavily on his mind. He had the strange and inexplicable feeling that somehow, from somewhere, he knew not where, something would simply turn up.

And turn up it did. In a way that Ebb could never have imagined. It happened early the following year. The long winter had finally spent the worst of its rage and its strength was beginning to wane. The first spring rains were starting to thaw out the land again. One morning, after a night of particularly heavy rain, the sun rose with a freshness and warmth that gave sweet fragrant promises of the spring to come. Ebb decided it would be a good day to take a walk around his land and see how it had survived the onslaughts of the winter. After some wandering he found himself climbing the hill towards the ancient apple tree to see if it had battled, life and limb, through the coldness to share another year of it's bounty with them.

From a distance he could see that the old tree was still standing and appeared strong and well. Then, still from some way off, he thought that he saw a flash of light from high up in the tree. The sun was only newly risen and sat low above the hills casting shallow angles of light upon the valley. Everything was still wet from the previous night's rains. He dismissed the glimmering as a trick of the light. Yet as he approached the tree more closely it happened again.

He stared curiously up into its branches, walking slowly round the trunk to see if he could find the source of this strange emission. Eventually he spotted the wooden shape of what had been the unpick-able apple high in the crown of the tree. The rain had soaked the wood. The warm spring sun had caused it to splinter and through the cracks there came sparkles of golden light.

He tried to examine more closely but it was too high for his poor eyes to discern any further details. He walked round the tree trying to view it from every angle but with no more success. Eventually he rushed excitedly back to the house to tell his daughters what he had seen and before long the whole family was climbing the hill with ladders in tow.

After a few moments fascinated staring the longest ladder was set firmly against the trunk of the tree and Issy began to climb. A moment latter she was stretched out on top of the ladder reaching towards the fruit that had so firmly refused to be picked the previous autumn. It came as quite a surprise to her when, with one gentle touch, the apple dropped neatly into her hand. She was however much more surprised when a light rub with her sleeve removed the soaked wooden coating to reveal a perfectly formed plump golden apple.

She almost fell backwards with the shock and had to steady herself against the ladder for a moment while she stared in wonder at this most precious of fruits. The eager shouts of her family below soon brought her back to her senses and hurrying down the ladder. After their gasps and exclamations had subsided Issy picked the golden apple up by the stork and, with great ceremony, placed it into her father's open palm.

...and as she did so four fine cracks appeared equally spaced around the fruit's golden surface; almost as if it were drying out in the warmth of his hand. Ebb raised his other hand to examine the fine cracks more closely and as he touched the top of the apple with his forefinger they opened out and the fruit fell apart.

The cracks were, in fact, slices that cut cleanly through to the core of the fruit, which had now fallen into four perfectly smooth and equally sized sections; and in the centre of each section sat a large golden seed.

Now Ebb understood the meaning of this peculiar phenomenon. On that mild autumn evening the previous year he had sat in the company of this old tree and his mind had been troubled. It seemed that the tree had heard his concerned plea for help and had responded with this magical gift.

The four sections of golden apple were the gifts that he would give to his four daughters on their wedding day. The slice of gold from the flesh of the fruit would in itself be enough to ensure that each daughter could live comfortably for a long time to come. It remained to be seen what wondrous things might be produced from such rare and magical seeds.

The business of the spring was soon upon them but Ebb's heart was light now. Whenever he wasn't working on the farm, preparing the land and sowing the new year's crops, he was involved in preparation for the weddings to come. News of the golden fruit had spread across the valleys like wild mint and there was a buzz of excitement in the air.

Everybody was looking forward to the feast of a lifetime but more than that they were keen to catch a glimpse of the quickly fabled slices of golden apple. Even in his business though Ebb made sure whenever he could to take the time to visit the old tree on the hill.

His gratitude was as deep as his joy. He promised himself that he would spend more time with the tree in the future. Soon he would need the company as much as the tree did.

The wedding day finally arrived. Everybody in Ebb's valley was invited. The four husbands arrived with their families and, on some pretext or another, virtually everybody from their home villages. The whether was fine and tables were laid out that covered a whole field by Ebb's house. It was understood in those days that performers and musicians were welcome at weddings and feasts The added excitement of the golden apple had spread news of these particular celebrations far and wide. Consequently the performers arrived in their droves and the feasting and the dancing went on long into the night.

The following morning four carts were piled high with grains and fruits and delicacies left over from the feast for the new brides to take away with them. Late in the morning, when all was packed and prepared, Ebb and his four daughters, their partners and families and a large contingency of onlookers climbed the hill to the ancient proud magical old apple tree.

Ebb told the crowd the story of the creation of the tree by Sky and Meadow (though they all knew it well) and the story of the events of the previous seasons from their autumn apple harvest to this year's rather unusual spring apple harvest. This story they all knew too but everybody was hungry for fresh new details that they could change and weave into a beautiful tapestry of images over the coming years. This fine yarn would eventually spin a life of it's own and would bear as much resemblance to the original as the summer does to the spring from which it is born.

Ebb then produced the four magical slices of apple for all to see. With words of blessing, of deep affection and of a true heartfelt love he presented one slice of the golden fruit to each of his daughters in turn.

After what seemed to Ebb like the briefest of moments all the good-byes were said, the tears were shed and his four daughters, their new families, half the wedding guests and their rare and wondrous dowries were off to begin their new lives.

During the course of the day the remainder of the wedding guests drifted back to their own homes. Some friends stayed late, talking, eating and helping to tidy (in that order). But by late that evening Ebb was alone on his farm for the first time in as long as he could remember. He sat in the quiet shell of his house with only an ancient apple tree on a near-by hill for company. Yet somehow he felt that the warmness in his heart and the memories and joy of the previous few days would see him through many winters to come.

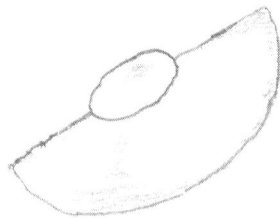

THE PLANTING

Ebb's daughters were received into their new villages with both the warmth of a long lost relative returning home and the fervour and excitement of visiting princesses. The morning after their arrivals, even before they began to unpack their possessions, they each went out into their respective gardens and filled a large pot with good quality earth. Then, thanking the old apple tree for its gifts, they placed the seeds on the soil, watered them lightly, covered them with another handful of soil and placed them in a warm spot in the fresh spring morning sunshine. This much they had agreed upon before they parted company and that they would check the seeds daily and tend what ever they produced with great care. As to what sprouted out of the seeds-, they could only wait to see.

They did not have to wait long though. For within a week the four daughters were watering four strong, vibrant seedlings. The young plants grew fast under such loving attention. The spring that year was as bright and warm as the winter had been deep and cold. By the summer the young plants had grown to a considerable size and each was beginning to display it's own unique characteristics. Another decision the daughters had taken was that, when the needs of these young plants became apparent, a place for planting them out would be carefully selected. And that this should be a public place. For it seemed to them that such rare and magical creatures should live in a place were all who needed them could find them.

Author's notes;

It should be said at this point that there is a degree of confusion concerning some of the details of the next part of the story. You see the four strong young plants eventually grew into large and impressive, but very different tress. It eventually became clear that each tree represented in its character the greatest virtue of the daughter who had planted it.

The trees (and sometimes the daughters too) were named by these characteristics. Since the names of the daughters bear obvious connections to those of the trees, many people have suggested that their original names have been forgotten. And that the names used below are simply corruptions of the qualities they refer to. Indeed the daughters and the trees were so closely associated that, in latter times, the four trees were often collectively referred to as "Ebb's daughters".

A similar point is the direction in which the daughter's villages lay, i.e. north, south, east and west. It has been said that this neatness is obviously a stylised representation of the cardinal points and thus the qualities associated with each; not truly where the four daughters lived. Some say in response that, in more magical times and especially in stories of the lives of people so clearly touched by magical forces, things simply had a way of working out poetically. Personally, I believe that it is impossible to separate the original details of a story as old as this from what it has come to mean.

Perhaps half of the value and beauty of these old tales comes from the way in which they have inter-woven with the lives of the people who have told them and changed accordingly.

What follows is an assemblage of the main threads that run through many of the oral traditions that lace the history of the four trees. I have also included information taken from an early botanical treatise on magical trees in which the trees referred to as "ebb's daughters" were covered extensively. Some of the language used here is of a technical nature but I have allowed this in the hope that, even if the odd word is passed over, this depth of detail will help to convey to the reader just how unique and magnificent these ancient trees really were.

The Tree of Wisdom

Isabel was the youngest and smallest of Ebbs daughter's but she had always displayed a wisdom beyond her years. Her way was gentle and humble and she was understanding and compassionate towards others. She was slight of body and fair of face with shortish mousy hair and pale blue eyes. Her heart was open and pure but her quiet bearing masked a deep inner strength. She was trusting in nature but would not tolerate anything dishonest or false. Above all she was wise. She seemed to have an innate understanding of the way things and people operated and she was always able to find the quickest and most harmonious solution to complicated situations or disputes. Thus the tree that she nurtured came to be known as the tree of wisdom

It was a small evergreen tree; the smallest of the four. With rounded deep green leaves covered in a thick waxy coating that was so shiny you could almost see your reflection in it. It was low growing and of unspectacular appearance, rounded in shape, looking like one of the most common of local trees. Were it not for the fact that it was planted alone in a place of noticeable beauty and for the subtle yet definite extra lustre to its leaves one would be forgiven for passing it by completely unnoticed.

The flowers came in the early winter months. They were small and ivy-like, cream in colour, deepening sometimes into a pale green. Around the edges of the petals was a fine border of speckled dark markings that looked at a glance like letters or writing in some strange unknown script. The flowers had a sweet subtle scent, though not very strong. The fruit followed in mid-winter. Small dark blue to black berries, like black-currents or sloes. It produced only a few fruit in stringy bunches. They had a very strong pungent earthy flavour that most people found unpalatable but some regarded as a great delicacy.

Isabel's village was three days walk north of her childhood home. The tree of wisdom was planted in the lee of a low south-facing hill a short distance from the village. It was a warm and comfortable spot which caught the sun well and even in the winter was a pleasant place to stop and spend a quiet moment.

People often came here in times of trouble to settle their minds or to clear their thoughts if they had an important decision to make. Some came here regularly just to soak in the atmosphere of the place and to be at peace. With time the tree and the hill were looked upon as a sacred spot in much the same way as the hill of the old apple tree was.

It was said that, if you had a problem or worry that you could not reconcile, you could go to the tree of wisdom in the early winter and pick one of its flowers. Then sit under the tree with the bloom in your hand and meditate upon the problem for some time. When your mind was settled and you felt a calmness within you should examine the flower carefully and you would be able to decipher the shapes around the edge of the petals and in this writing you would find the answer to your troubles.

The Tree of Joy

The next oldest of Ebb's daughters was called Joy. And she was well named indeed. She was a vivacious, colourful young woman. Always full of life and happiness, always glad to help people and always surrounded by laughter. It seemed as if waves of lightness and happiness rippled out from around her wherever she went; just as the waves might ripple across the surface of a great still lake if somebody were to wade in the shallows of one of it's banks.

Like her, the tree of joy was tall and proud. It had large pale green deciduous leaves with a flamboyant, whitish, poplar-like under-surface that flashed in the sunlight whenever the leaves were tossed by the wind.
It was upright in posture. It's trunk thick and standard and it's long, slender branches reached for the heavens with all their hearts.

It flowered in the spring and the flowers were truly spectacular. The sizeable five-petalled blooms were born from bright yellow bract-like sepals, which lasted as long as the flowers. The underside of the petals was a vivid pink while the upper surface was a soft lilac, which faded through mauve to a rich deep purple as the flower aged.

The stamens were large and colourful. The anthers varied from ochre to bright orange, and they often produced so much pollen that, in certain warm, damp conditions, this would dye many of the trees leaves with streaks of flaming sunrise. And, just in case the flowers had so far escaped your attention, the massive swollen carpels were a deep royal blue. Thus, the overall effect of the tree in full flower was that of an enormous living, dancing, constantly changing rainbow.

Joy's new home was on the main street of a bustling market village three days walk to the east of her father's land. The tree of joy was planted in the centre of the village green and was a focal point for celebrations of all kinds. In particular the "welcoming of the spring" festival. On the eve of May, people gathered here from afar for it was considered great fortune to be able to celebrate the Beltaine feast in the presence of this tree.

That night fires were lit and musicians played and people danced until dawn. Few slept on the eve of May. The whole of the following day was spent feasting and playing. The tree of joy was decorated with charms containing peoples wishes for the coming year and then covered, as part of a dance, with brightly coloured ribbons; as if it was not quite colourful enough of it's own accord.

This tree's extravagance did not end there though because the fruits that followed were a show in their own right. It seems that, when the explanation as to how and why a tree should choose the form and colour of its fruit was given, this tree was obviously not present. Or else, it was so filled with the joy of the creative possibilities of fruit making that it found the idea of producing the same fruit twice almost impossibly tedious. Consequently, each fruit that the tree produced, and it produced many, was entirely different.

They varied in size from tiny berries to huge swollen pumpkins. They ranged in colour from white to black and through every colour of the rainbow on the way. They might be soft in texture or hard, pithy, segmented, smooth or even crunchy. And the skin could be as fine as silk and pleasantly palatable, or rough and inedible. In shape they could be as round as an orange, as long and thin as a banana, or any of a range of shapes that cannot be compared to modern fruits, including some with spikes, some with holes in the middle, flat disc-shaped ones and some that were almost square.

And the variety did not end there because their flavour was as unpredictable as their form. Some were tangy as lemons, some as soft as a pear. Some were as sweet as a fresh ripe mango, while others were as tart as early gooseberries. It is said also that some were fizzy like sherbet when properly ripened and that others were quite savoury. The only feature they all seemed to share was that they were all truly delicious. Of course, the great diversity of flavours meant that it was impossible to cook with or preserve the fruit in any way. But this never was a problem because, usually at harvest time, there was such a great gathering of people wanting to eat them fresh that few survived long enough to need storing.

Sometimes the tree of joy produced fruit that were replicas of those of its sister trees, or were even exaggerated versions of them, as if in mock humour. The only form that occurred regularly was that of the apple. Every year, without fail, the tree of joy produced one large beautifully formed apple. This was thought to be as a sign of gratitude and respect to its parent plant and the local people always found a special purpose for this most precious fruit.

Many traditions grew around the apple of joy, as it was known. It could be presented to an individual who had accomplished a feat of great worth, or had given selfless service to others. Sometimes it was given back to the earth as an offering of thanks after a good harvest. One tradition was that it would be baked into a huge pie with normal apples and this was shared out between all the village members at the mid-winter festival. A piece was always left under the tree for the wild animals to take in the night. This was said to render favour with the spirits of nature and encourage good harvests in the future.

So the tree called Joy lived at the heart of its community, as did the woman who shared its name and both of their long lives were filled with happiness and light and were remembered with affection long after their passing.

The Tree of Love

The third of Ebb's daughters was called Violet and she was truly lovely, in both appearance and in spirit. She had a warm, generous heart that could soften any anger and calm any storm. She had an ease of being that endeared her to all those who knew her and could befriend any stranger; and she had a grace and natural elegance that was the stuff of poetry.

A true and rare beauty was Violet. Her hair was mahogany, her eyes teak, her skin was olive and her smile golden. Her face was amiable and pleasantly rounded yet her features were as fine as a crescent moon or a new china tea set and her lips were as red as any rose. She moved with the grace of a ballet dancer and a wild cat combined, her eyes sparkled with joy and friendship and her touch was soft as a summer breeze.

From a young age heads had turned when she passed by, so it surprised many that she had not married earlier. Indeed, there had been no shortage of offers. She had attracted suitors from far afield, the wealthy, the brave, the charming and the handsome. Many had vied for the hand of Violet, yet all she had gently declined.

Violet was unimpressed by the things of the world. Only true love would ever move her heart and now, late in her life, she had found it; and in the finding the radiance of her beauty had blossomed into a fullness beyond compare. Her husband was a local man of no great wealth and unremarkable appearance whom some considered a rather poor catch but he was strong and true and their love was real, and when they were together all those who saw them were touched by their tenderness and affection.

Violet's home was three day's walk to the south of Ebb's farm. It was a picturesque little village nestled into the foot of a large hill on which there stood the ruins of an old castle. In earlier times the castle had been an impressive fortress and the village had been the lively centre of local commerce. Now the village was a shadow of it's former self and the hilltop stronghold little more than a pile of rocks and rubble inhabited mostly by sheep.

On the lower slopes of the south side of the hill were the remnants of an old walled garden. This too was a feint echo of its earlier glory but it retained a sense of mystery and atmosphere. The forest had encroached up to the walls on two sides and much of the inside was covered with briars but a few of the more exotic introduced plants had survived. There were a variety of unusual herbs and spices fighting for space amongst the native ones. There was also a number of rare and unnameable trees trying desperately to shake the brambles from their lower branches and on the north wall a couple of delicate double flowered hybrid roses were keeping pace with the dogs.

The walls of the garden had taken the years well and stood strong and firm. Many of the ornamental paths, which once crisscrossed the garden in a formal design, had survived too. So despite its general neglect and untidiness it was thought of fondly by the locals. It was a favourite place for couples to wander on warm summer evenings drinking in the sweet, spicy smells of the herbs and looking at the roses. It was a treasure throve of medicines for the local wise women and had played "secret garden" to most of the village children at some point in their lives.

Violet decided that this would be the ideal spot for her tree. She cleared an area in the Northeast corner of the garden so that the tree could soak in the sun's rays until they sank out of sight and then snuggle into the warm walls for the night. She also hoped that by planting such a special tree here it would give a new lease of life to the garden, and in this, she was right. Within a few years of the new planting the garden began to thrive again. People cleared many of the briars, cleaned what remained of the pathways and restored some of the ornamental wooden benches.

This attention was more casual and haphazard however than the disciplined work the garden had demanded in its heyday so it retained some of the softness of age. Perhaps the clean freshness of youth would have looked odd on such a mature garden. Anyway, the tree and the garden grew strong and vibrant together. The tree ripened into the prime of its life and the garden, mentor-like, enjoyed the second flowering of old age. Together their joint beauty enriched all who visited them.

The tree of love was a stately tree indeed. Its large majestic boughs stretched out low from the trunk like open arms waiting to embrace you as you approached. Its stature was grand and full-bodied as if hugging the earth and reaching for the sky at the same time. The leaves were large and evergreen and soft to the touch. They were covered with a thick coat of fine silky hairs that gave them a texture like velvet and those that had fallen lay on the ground beneath the tree giving it a covering as rich as any carpet.

The tree of love flowered, as you might expect, in the height of summer and its flowers were as beautiful as those of the tree of joy were extravagant. They were large and many petalled. At first, they appeared like deep red roses. The smaller outer petals opened first into several inter-playing layers around the larger central petals which were all red on the outside. But this was only half the flower's beauty because the blossoms only fully opened at night.

When the nights were warm and still, the moon full and high and the air was filled with the delicate aromas of meadow herbs, then the tree of love came into full bloom. Once the large inner petals had opened out and arched themselves backwards to stare at the stars, the red of the flower could no longer be seen and the blossom was completely transformed.

The blooms did not open flat but remained slightly funnel shaped. The central petals seemed much larger when fully opened and their inner face was a soft creamy magnolia, which called to the full moon as if it were a kindred soul and glowed dustily in it's light. The colour of the petals deepened rapidly towards the base so that all the central core of the bloom, including the stamen and carpels, was black as night. This gave the flower the impression that it was much deeper than it was but the final feature of this enchanting flower was its spots.

These were tiny and sparse, not every blossom had spots and few had more the three or four but they were a brilliant iridescent blue green colour which glowed like some strange deep-sea fish; or a dance of bioluminescent bacteria. Within the blossom itself the effect was like looking into a deep midnight ocean and catching brief glimpses of the bizarre and exotic creatures that reside there, hidden and unknowable.

From a distance however the sight of the tree of love in flower was sublime. The hundreds of sparkling spots became the great band of the Milky Way crossing a night sky with a thousand moons… Or perhaps it was a myriad of tiny stars shimmering above a meadow of summer flowers… Or maybe the sparkling eyes of other worldly beings as they laboured over a garment for some distant heavenly queen. However you perceived it, the effect was enthralling and people often stood in the middle of the night and watched the flowering tree for hours.

The fruits came late in the summer or early fall and were the reverse of the flowers in colour. When they first appeared they were a brilliant, dazzling white. The pure, luminous white of a unicorn catching rays of sunlight in a forest of shadow and gloom. As they filled out to their full size (and they were sizeable fruits) their colour softened to the earthier, grainy shades of a Hebridean white sand beach. But when the fruit were fully ripe they took on the soft creaminess of a newly risen full moon.

Sometimes they even developed pale grey patches over the skin, which increased their lunar resemblance no end.

When they were cut open the inner flesh of the fruit was a rich sensuous red, somewhere between strawberry and cherry, with perhaps a stirring of watermelon. It had the texture of ice cream and the fragrance of lychee and bananas. To compare its flavour with any other fruit would not do it justice. For it was unlike any other that you may have tasted. It was as refreshing as a drink of water from a cool mountain spring on a hot summer's walk. Yet as comforting as an open fire on a winter's night. It had a zest that spoke of life and adventure, yet was as soothing and nurturing as a welcome home after a long hard day. It was fulsome and earthy, yet deliciously invigorating, and altogether as sweet as clover honey.

The flavour of this fruit could only be appreciated by experiencing it and every year crowds gathered to do just that. Despite the fact that consuming such a magical substance carried certain risks (as you will see) not a single mouthful was ever wasted. In the middle of the fruit was a large flat seed. They were red brown in colour with ornately detailed patterns in the grain of their wooden coating and all were perfectly heart-shaped. They were beautifully smooth objects that were always warm to the touch; as if they liked being held and perhaps because they did not wither or dry out many people valued them more highly than the fruit itself.

As you can imagine, there are no end of fables and myths surrounding this most magical of trees. For example, a couple had only so much as to pass underneath one of its branches hand in hand and they were sure to fall instantly and desperately in love. You can also probably imagine therefore that there was a regular stream of young men and women trying, equally desperately, to get other young women and men to walk under one of this tree's branches while holding their hand. To spend a night with somebody under this tree was as good as a marriage and was considered thus by the local people.

A couple who wanted children but had so far been unsuccessful were advised to lay together under the tree of love on a full moon night, particularly when the tree was in flower where they were sure to conceive. It was said that if you slept under the tree of love alone for the three nights of the full moon then you were sure to meet your true love before the moon was full again. This however could be a risky occupation for, if somebody else had the same idea, or perhaps if you had an overly keen admirer, you might wake one of these three mornings to find yourself quite married.

The fruit was also considered magically aphrodisiac and herein lay part of its danger. For though its flavour was most delicious, its flesh was so filling that it was very difficult for one person to consume a whole fruit. It does not take too much thought to guess what the possible consequences of sharing a fruit of this nature with somebody might be. Suffice to say that a number of oddly matched couples resulted from those who were not careful in the choice of dinner partner.

The seeds were prized as gifts and talismans. They were threaded on necklaces and presented to loved-ones on special anniversaries or sent on Valentines Day by half-anonymous admirers. They were worn proudly as broaches by happily married women and men; almost as wedding bands are worn today. They were given to anybody going on a long journey by partners or family members to remind them of the love that waited for them at home. Sometimes they were just carried in the pocket or purse and rubbed for good luck or luckiness in love. However they were used they were always cherished by their owners and regarded as things of lightness and joy.

Most of the tales that grew around the tree of love are sweet summer stories with happily-ever-after endings but there are a few, particularly those that concern the fearie folk, that touch upon the darker side of love. The story that follows warns that it is possible to loose oneself completely when love is too strong.

I include some of it here because it is one of my favourites.

The Fearie Queen

Once upon a time when the forests behind castle hill stretched as far as the eyes could see and further than any man had ever walked there lived a fearie queen. Queen she was but happy she was not. Many years earlier her husband, the king, whom she had never truly loved, had been killed in a battle with his brother. The queen had refused to help him win the battle. So, in his dying breath he had cursed her, saying from that time on that she would only be able to fall in love with mortal men.

At first this did not seem to her to be such an awful curse for, shortly afterwards, she did indeed fall deeply in love with a mortal man. With her skill and her beauty she enticed him into the fearie realm and there they were married. She lavished her wealth upon him and they both drank deeply from the cup of pleasure and eat their fill of the fruits of new love. But being a mortal man he was destined to grow old and when he did her sweet fruit turned sour. Before long she tired of his frailty and weakness and she cast him harshly out of her queendom.

He could not find his way back to the mortal world alone and so he was deprived of the release of death's sweet sleep. He was doomed to wander through the fearie lands for the rest of time suffering the illnesses and pains of old age. She had now realised the strength of the curse; that no love would ever last for her and she must always seek for something that she could never find.

Later in this story her yearning eye falls upon a woodsman who lived alone in a log cabin deep in the forest. His name was Cedar and he was strong and handsome. His hair was black as the raven's wings and his eyes as blue as the midday sky and the fearie queen thought, as she always did, that he was the most beautiful man she had ever seen.

She watched him from a distance for seven days and seven nights and then, early one clear spring morning, she approached him. The sun was newly risen in the east and the newly waxing moon tailed invisibly behind, hidden from view by its brightness. The fearie queen appeared to Cedar in the form of a young girl with two long plaits of fair hair hanging down to her waist. She told him that she was an orphan who had been wandering through the forest in search of a new home and asked if she might stay with him until she could find somebody to care for her.

Cedar felt pity for the child but he was a man of the earth and was not fooled quite so easily. He was pure hearted and hard working and he saw the world very clearly. He examined her closely for a moment before he replied and he could see a very subtle shimmer of light around her outline. It was like a fine heat haze over a summer field, so fine that it would have escaped all but the truest eye. But Cedar recognised it and he knew her to be fey and he sent her away.

She came to him next when the summer was hot. On a bright, butterfly filled afternoon the day before the full moon she found him working outside in the sun. This time she appeared as a beautiful young woman in the flowering of her life. Her hair was loose and her gown flowed freely on the gentle July breeze. She wore a garland of meadow flowers around her neck and carried a basket of red roses on her soft white arm.

She asked if he wanted to buy one of her roses. He told her that he owned no money. She replied that he could pay her with a kiss and fluttered her long eyelashes coyly. He looked longingly at her soft red lips and his solitude ached for her company but again his eyes were true. He lived always with honesty as his friend and could not be thrown by a veil of beauty drawn over a web of deceit.

So, for the second time he saw through her illusion and sent her away.

In the fall, she tried once more. This time she came late in the day when the sun was sinking into the trees in the west, the out-shined waning moon having already retired. She took the form of a wise old hag dressed in rags, weighed down with necklaces and charms. She removed a bundle from inside her cloak and spread it on the ground in front of him. A strange assortment of objects jostled for his attention. From things of obvious rarity and value to things that looked as if they had just been picked up off the path plus one or two things that his eyes could make no sense of at all.

With words as playful as any poem, in tones as lilting as any song she captured his thoughts... and there she painted the story of her art. She told him of the potions that she could concoct and the spells that she could cast which would grant him anything that his heart desired. She offered him riches beyond imagining and power beyond his dreams. Upon the open loom of his trusting mind she wove a vivid tapestry of fame and success, adventure and passion.

Yet, when she had finished and he was allowed a moment to decide which of these wondrous things he desired most, he realised that he needed none of them. He was in fact, and had always been, deeply contented with his life in the forest and he knew now that the simplicity and peace that he enjoyed here was a gift of greater value than any that the old lady could offer him. In this realising he recognised her for who she was and he stood up without a word, walked into his house and closed the door behind him.

He thought that he would not see her again but he was wrong for she came a fourth time. This time she came in the dead of winter when the moon was black. She knocked on his door long after sunset on the day of his birth and this time she came as herself- the fearie queen. He opened the door to her and she smiled at him. For the first time it was a genuine smile, her own smile to him. She told him that she was sorry for trying to trick him into loving her. She begged for his forgiveness and as an offering of peace and friendship she had baked him a sweet pie for his birthday.

This was the only day in the year when his solitude snapped at his ankles like a puppy dog craving affection. All day long his heart had been heavy at the thought of spending his special day alone in this dark wintry wood. He longed for the lightness of conversation and the simple joy of sharing, and so, against his better judgement, he invited her in. He shared his evening meal with her and she embroidered tales of her fearie palace onto his eager countenance. When they had finished the meal she sang an entrancing fearie birthday song to him and then she cut the cake.

The cake was a sweet pastry stuffed full of the baked fruits from the tree of love. Before Cedar had finished one slice of it, he had risen to his feet. Without a backward glance he left his cabin and his tools behind him and followed the fearie queen into another world and was never seen again.

The Tree of Rest

Theresa was Ebb's oldest daughter and she was a healer. She was a peaceful woman with a gentle smile. She had a harmonious way about her that overflowed and filled the air around her with a sense of well being. She had long dark hair and a friendly beaming round face with eyes that sparkled. From her early childhood she had been blessed with the gift of hands and she had always eagerly sought out the company of the village wise women. From these she had learned the ways of herbs and medicines and of healing songs. She showed great promise in these arts and had quickly learned all the local healers could teach her.

When she was a young woman a wandering holyman passed through their valley. For three weeks he stayed in Ebb's house while Theresa plied him with questions and drank his answers as thirstily as a person who has been wandering in a desert drinks when they finally reach an oasis. He taught her about the movements of the sun and the moon, the planets and the stars. He taught her philosophies and ways of healing from far-off lands. He told that it was possible to tell a persons state of health just by examining the whites of their eyes, and to predict a person's future form the patterns in the palm of their hands. Many strange and marvellous things he taught her and she listened intently and remembered well.

Since that time her knowledge was valued highly by all who knew her and as she grew older and wiser people would come to her from far afield to seek cures for their ailments and advise on their troubles. After she married, she moved west where the sun sets to a small farming village just a few miles from the coast. She lived a short distance outside the village on the farm that her husband had inherited from his forefathers and together they reared a large family of their own. There was a small room at the side of the house which Theresa used like a surgery. Here she prepared her medicines and most days one or two or more people would come to seek her counsel.

She mixed pills for all ills and life saving salves
from simples for pimples to balms for bruised arms
from refreshing lotions to untangle the emotions
to magical potions for more fiery commotions
medicinal dresses eased all manner of messes
as gentle compresses calmed children's distresses

She practiced spiritual healing to connect with deep feelings
and hands on massage for the rigours of age
brewed concoctions and decoctions for all their afflictions
with herbal infusions to iron out confusions
cooked ointments and creams to ward off bad dreams
and tonic brews for chronic flues

She healed cats and dogs, pet rats and frogs
cattle and horses, birds and sheep
and could waken a madman from out of his ravings
feed him wise words then send him soundly to sleep

In front of their house a busy stream flowed down towards the sea. Behind them the land rose gently to a west-facing hill. This was covered in a neat patchwork of woodland and meadow. At one point there was a clearing in a small wood were it was possible to see down the path cut into the hills by the stream and catch glimpses of the sea. Theresa thought this would be a good home for her tree. It was a quiet, nurturing spot that was often bathed in soft orange light at sunset. A good place to spend time alone and yet it was not so far from the village that people would find it difficult to get there. At certain times of the year, whether permitting, it was possible to see the sun set into the sea from here.

The tree of rest, or the tree of healing- as it was sometimes known was a most individual creature. It had a thick straight trunk which bore no branches at all for the first six or eight feet. Then a whole array of huge branches sprouted out umbrella-like all at once. These stretched out horizontally for a great distance until, under the strain of their own weight, they bowed back down to touch the ground. The tree's higher branches had a similar habit and lay criss-crossed over the lower ones to form a complete canopy.

The effect of this peculiar growth was that the space under the tree was like a large, well-roofed room with one massive central pillar. The leaves on the tree were long and thin like a willow's but so deeply serrated that they looked more like feathers than leaves. They were pale-green in colour and grew so thickly on the branches that they over-locked each other and made the roof of this living room quite waterproof. The leaves were also so rich in essential oils that the whole tree and the area around it were constantly infused with a fresh soothing aroma.

The tree of rest was deciduous, but not quite in the normal way. That is to say, it shed its leaves every year, not early in the winter as most trees did, but rather in the early summer. The tree rested in the winter and did not use the old leaves, but they remained firmly attached to its branches thus maintaining a waterproof roof. In the spring a new set of fresh, pale green feathers was produced and it was not until these were fully opened that the old ones were allowed to fall. Also, unlike most trees, this tree did not remove all its precious oils from its spent leaves but allowed them to remain there.

Since the old leaves fell in the dry, stillness of early summer into the bowels of a tree were no wind ever stirred, they collected there year after year. Over the long life of the tree layer upon layer of these scented feather-like leaves had piled on top of each other to form a thick bed as soft as any down stuffed cushion. This was infused with the sweet aroma of the most healing and fragrant essential oils which reminded one of a cross between camphor, eucalyptus, lavender soap, and freshly washed sheets.

The stronger smell of the new leaves on the branches was a balm that could lift any headache, soothe any care and loosen any knot merely in the smelling. It made the breath flow more easily, caused the mind to quieten and wander to picnic pleasant thoughts and it induced a general sense of well being that was halfway between sleep and wakefulness, half way between dreaming and listening to a children's story.

The tree of rest flowered in the autumn. Its flowers were beautiful but only in the way that flowers normally are, not the sublime beauty of the flowers of her sister, the tree of love. They were born on long pendulous bracts that hung down into the dimness of the living-room below. The bracts were a pale sky blue, which glowed, eerily in the dull light of the space beneath the branches.

The flowers came out two or three at a time, starting at the top of the bract and spiralling down to its tapered end. Each flower had six rich purple petals, which seemed slightly too large for the space they were allowed, and ruffled up ornamentally. They lived for several days and then, as the flowers below them began to bloom, they faded to a pale pink colour and dropped onto the soft bed below, adding their colour and scent to the mattress of feather leaves.

The fruit of the tree of rest were most unusual. They were produced in scattered swirls on the hanging bracts when all the flowers had dropped in the late autumn or early winter. But they did not behave like most other fruits, which ripen and then fall when their season has passed. These fruit remained on the tree until they were harvested, even if that took a year or more. So, there were always fruit waiting to be consumed on this tree, whatever the season

Their appearance was also quite unique. At first sight, they resembled spiralling cluster of tiny coconuts, each about the size of a large plum or small apricot. They had hard, brown woody shells with thin cream-coloured veins, and a thick coating of coarse hairs that looked like fine hedgehog quills. Each was attached to the bract by a short woody stalk and to harvest them you held this stalk tightly in one hand, grasped the bottom of the fruit firmly in the other and gave it a swift twist.

The stalk remained attached to the tree and held a small section of the top of the fruit with it, like the slice one removes from a hard-boiled egg with a teaspoon. So the section of fruit that came free was now like a rounded small-mouthed cup and in it was the true magic of this tree. The contents of the fruit were entirely liquid, like the milk of a coconut, except that it was a soft creamy pink in colour. Each fruit contained about one mouthful of this precious juice whose flavour was said to be sweeter than any nectar.

It tasted of honey and camomile and dancing angels, of lazy days spent floating on a river of butterflowers, or boating across a sea of dreams. The fragrance of this delicious elixir was a mixture of so many things that it was impossible to take them all in once and almost compelled you to sit down and explore it at length, savouring every nuance, drifting idly upon waves of sweet-scented sensations.

It had the brightness and joy of spring flowering gorse or of a hawthorn tree in may, yet the sweetness of wild honeysuckle in a still summer wood. It had the freshness and freedom of heather and ling, scoots pine and juniper growing on a wind brushed autumnal mountainside, yet the delicacy of a surprise January rose, and throughout, the fullness and body of winter flowering jasmine.

The list of medicinal properties attributed to the ambrosial milk of the tree of rest is a long one indeed and the list of ailments and maladies it is said to have cured is neigh-on endless. In truth, every part of this tree was rich in healing virtues. The leaves were nervine, used to sedate people suffering from insomnia or from shock or intense stress. The flowers were very cleansing and tonic, a herb tea was sometimes made to help those who had been seriously ill to return to full health. Even the bark was valued as a strong painkiller.

Most of the local healers had small stocks of these substances but they tended to use them only after all other treatments had been tried. This was partly because they were very strong and partly because their effect was magical as well as medicinal and therefore could be unpredictable. But mostly it was because it was not considered appropriate to take samples from the body of such a rare tree, especially when it freely offered a juice that generally did the job better anyway. Simply spending time with this tree, breathing in its essential oils and bathing in it's healing atmosphere was often enough to cure a minor ailment and induce a peaceful state of mind. Where the need was greater then the contents of the sweet magical cup of health were consumed and the tree was allowed to weave its magic.

This divine drink was the last word in healing. When the wise women had tried all their herbs and the medicine men had tested all their potions and a patient remained uncured then they were advised to visit the tree of healing. Many came on pilgrimage to this tree from great distances to drink its magical elixir and rest under its fragrant branches. One fruit was enough. People were strongly advised not to consume more than one fruit in any given year and few tasted this powerful cocktail more than three times in their life.

Once the milk was consumed a deep healing sleep was soon induced. Some would sleep for a week or more, others would wake after a while then just lie still and rest, breathing deeply and gazing into an imaginary landscape of colourful birds and fishes and nameless heavenly beings. All those who supped from the fruit of the tree of rest emerged refreshed and rejuvenated. Many were cured completely; all were greatly improved. Nobody left this sanctuary of health without a feeling of lightness and well-being, and none ever returned with the same problem.

These were the four trees that people came to know as Ebb's daughters and the four women after whom they were named. Long and full were their lives, many were their gifts, and blessed were all those who knew them.

THE HARVEST

Again the world turned, the land yawned and sighed and the people changed. Ebb's daughters returned to their mother's side and, for a time, their daughters and their grand daughters kept their memories alive. Then they too passed, turned like waves into the folds of the years. The memories became stories and the stories grew strong, like a clinging vine growing round the branches of time, twisting and stretching, always reaching for the light of each new dawn.

When more generations had passed than there are fish in a shoal or ants in a hill and the stories had changed so much that some parts had come full circle and began to resemble the truth again; in the village that had once been the home of Isabel, there lived a woman called Mary. She was directly descended from Isabel in a line of great-great grand daughters, or so she said. This was said so often though that it became a figure of speech, which meant something in-between "my family have lived in these parts for a long time" and "I'm a person of good breeding".

Mary had lived a long and happy life and was respected and loved by her neighbours and kin. Like Issy, she was known for her gentleness and her wisdom which was perhaps another reason why she was associated with that most renowned of local benefactors. She was also a great lover of the tree of wisdom and spent lots of time sitting under its boughs, meditating on the daily events of the village and contemplating the deeper streams of life.

One day, after some hours spent sitting quietly under the tree listening to the wind and watching her thoughts, she opened her eyes very slowly, almost unintentionally. In this soft, peaceful state the veil of familiarity was lifted and she saw the tree anew, as if she were seeing it for the first time. What she noticed came to her as quiet a surprise.

For she realised that the tree of wisdom was growing old. This tree had stood peaceful and strong on the side of this hill for time out of memory. It had been such an integral part of her life and a part of the culture of her ancestors for so long that it had never occurred to anybody before that a time might come when it was no longer here. It was undoubtedly a magical tree, as were its sisters, but that did not mean that it was immortal.

Running on the heals of this realisation, it occurred to Mary that none of the four magical trees had ever produced any offspring. They were all abundant producers of seeds, but none of these had been known to germinate. She decided that something must be done about this situation. Certainly these trees should not be simply allowed to die out if there was anything that could be done to help them remain.

At first she was unsure how she could help because she didn't really understand why such generous and giving creatures should be apparently so infertile. She decided that the best way of finding out the answer to this problem was to consult the tree itself. Though the whether was mild, it was winter and the tree of wisdom was in flower. These flowers that had been such a source of inspiration and guidance for so many generations of her people she would use now for the benefit of the tree that bore them.

She gently plucked a nearby bloom then she sat still leaning her back against the trunk of the tree, breathing softly and calming her mind. When her thoughts were at peace and her spirit was clear she opened her eyes slowly for a second time and allowed them to rest upon the flower. She had done this many times in her life before today; searching for solutions to her own or other's problems. Each time the process had been the same.

First she would see a small but beautiful flower in the palm of her hand, then slowly as she allowed her eyes to relax and her mind to wander she would begin to discern shapes in the delicate black markings round the edges of its petals. After a while the shapes became clearer and she began to be able to read them. Mostly they were words of inspiration, pure and sublime. Sometimes they were instruction and occasionally they referred to the problem at hand quite specifically.

This time however the experience was very different. The moment she opened her eyes to look at the flower she heard a voice speaking clearly in her thoughts. The voice was strong and definite but it was a kind voice and she was not startled. Somehow she knew immediately that it was the voice of the tree and, since she considered the tree to be an old friend, there was nothing to fear. The voice had a soothing almost hypnotic quality which settled into such a rhythm that Mary felt as though she could listen to it forever.

A long tale it told her that day which began before the birth of the ancient Apple tree on Ebb's land. The voice told her of the ordering of the gods and goddesses and of the creation of the world and all the creatures on it. It told her the ways of plants and animals and men and their relationship to each other. And it sang to her the songs of the land which had been taught to it by the divine beings who had held this knowledge since the dawn of the world.

Mary lost herself in the mystery of these words and the beauty of the images drawn before her. Afterwards she could not have said whether she listened for a few short hours or for a lifetime or more. Eventually the tree began to speak of its own life and of that of its sisters and here Mary became more wakeful, for she new this part of the story concerned her.

Finally, the voice explained why the four trees had born no fertile fruit. It went like this. It was the way of things that everything must change and some day pass away completely. The trees of the earth had but a short life-span and then they died; so, if they chose to, they were allowed to self-pollinate. Since any form of reproduction was by its nature imperfect these trees would change slightly with every generation and all was well.

The four trees of Ebb's daughters, on the other hand, had such vast life-spans that the ability to self-seed would have granted them virtual immortality and this was something the gods were fiercely jealous of. They were of coarse allowed to cross-pollinate with other trees in order to reproduce because this would produce a distinct and new variety of tree with each generation and so the goddess of change would be satisfied.

But here was their problem. Being purely magical trees they were not yet able to cross-pollinate with the trees of the earth. Of course, all trees were originally born as unique magical beings but most of the species that grew on the earth these days were so old that their sap lines had diverged beyond recognition and they were no longer compatible. Technically, the four trees could only cross breed with each other but since they were so widely separated this had not happened. They could also cross with first generation magical trees from other parts of the world but this was obviously even less likely to happen.

Now Mary understood the problem and, in so doing, she understood both the solution to the problem and the purpose to the rest of her life. She knew straight away that she would devote the rest of her days to propagating the four trees known as Ebb's daughters and she would plant out as many of the resulting offspring as the years would allow her to. In this way she hoped to repay some of the service that the tree of wisdom had given her through her life and had given to the people of her land for countless ages.

Thanking the tree for the gifts of knowledge that it had imparted to her in its story, she stood up and began her life's work that very day. Firstly, she folded a leaf from the tree into the shape of a small envelope then she carefully collected pollen from as many flowers as she could reach until her package was quite stuffed. Later, at home she stored this pollen safely in a glass vial and then returned to the tree with more containers. With the help of a few short ladders and three or four of her grandchildren she filled nine glass vials with the precious pollen from the tree of wisdom.

The following spring she set out to visit the village where the tree of joy lived. She arrived there the last week in April and stayed with a distant cousin of hers whom she had not seen for some years. She had with her three of the vials containing pollen from the tree of wisdom and a small bag-full of jars to collect pollen from the notoriously abundant tree of joy.

It was decided that both the pollination and the collection should be incorporated into the May Day celebrations so Mary spent the next few days teaching a small group of local children the art of pollination. She taught them about the history of all the magical trees, their personalities and how to care for them. She told them stories of the origins of the world and of all the plants and animals and peoples on it; and together they worked the pollination into a dance which recounted some of the important events in the life of their special tree.

From its magical beginnings right up to the present day and this most auspicious of maydays they danced and as they decorated the tree with coloured ribbons, so they dusted it with the pollen from the tree of wisdom. As they hung their gifts and charms upon its boughs, so they filled the glass jars with copious amounts of its flamboyant orange pollen.

Mary returned home happy and satisfied. As well as doing a job that gave her immense pleasure it was turning into a year of great celebration; both for her and for everybody who loved the trees.

In the summer, her work began in earnest. Now she journeyed south to the village where the tree of love grew. She carried three vial of pollen from the tree of wisdom, a dozen empty vials to collect pollen from the tree of love, and two jars of pollen from the tree of joy. There was no main festival associated with the tree of love in summer so she worked here in a more orderly manner. This was useful because she wanted to fertilise half of the flowers with pollen from the tree of wisdom and half with pollen from the tree of joy. She also wanted to label each flower so that she could collect the seeds individually and have an idea of which two trees had produced them.

A few locals displayed an interest in her work and these were given the job of watching over the tree and the labelled flowers during this delicate time. Then Mary travelled to the Northeast, back to the tree of joy to collect the fruits from the flowers that she had pollinated there in the spring. As was often the case in the village that housed the tree of joy this proved to take much longer than she had anticipated and involved much more fun and celebration than was strictly required.

The fruiting time of the tree of joy did not have a specific day associated with it as the flowering time did, mainly because the tree fruited for so long. Since each fruit was completely different they all ripened at different rates. It was a great art and a source of pride, as well as many local competitions and games, to be able to tell exactly when a particular fruit was ready to eat.

Consequently, there was a mildly festive air here throughout the summer. With people coming and going in disordered groups, taking part in the games and competitions A whole flurry of activity revolved around the tree of joy through the summer time. With all the local traders that arrived to feed the visitors and the wandering minstrels who gathered to entertain them the population of the village was almost doubled.

The whether was fine that year. People were camped out all over the village green and in the gardens of friends and relatives. Mary stayed with her cousin again and with the help of her extended family and a small army of local children news was spread about her wish to collect all the seeds she could. And, as was the way in this village, a number of fun and interesting ways were thought up to encourage people to comply. Mary set up a stall on the village green near the tree where she could collect the seeds and this was manned or womanned continuously.

As well as the seeds, she was also keen to have descriptions of the fruit from which they came. Thanks to some donations from a few of the village elders a competition was organised which offered prizes to those who gave the fullest and most accurate descriptions of the fruit they had eaten. These were expected to include details of the fruit's size, flavour, shape and texture, as well as any peculiarities, such as "long time ripening", or "numerous spiny thorns", or "flesh changed colour after fruit was opened". A prize was also given for the best adult and the best child's drawing of any fruit.

The summer was bright and joyous; filled with laughter and dancing children and seemed to Mary to pass all too quickly. By the end of it she had acquired a veritable catalogue of seeds and a complete portfolio of drawings, paintings and eloquent longwinded description of their respective fruits. Some were like high school essays, some were like fearie stories or fantastic legends built around the day of picking the fruit, or the competition in which it was won, or the journey to the village.

Others were like a complete life history of the person who picked the fruit from the moment of birth and some even stretched back to cover their ancestors. Mary loved them all and it amused her no end to think that she had originally imagined herself returning home with a packet of seeds, or perhaps a small bag of them. She obviously had not included the people of the village of joy in her equation.

Back at home she set about ordering the massive amount of information she had collected into a manageable form. Then she carefully labelled what seemed like an enormous number of clay pots and set the appropriate seed, or seeds in each. These were placed in a cold frame that her eldest daughter's husband had built for her at the bottom of her garden in case the winter was severe. She barely had this task finished when it was time to set off again on her quest. This time was headed south and west to the tree of rest.

She arrived there early in the autumn. Just in time to see the first delicate purple blooms stretch and yawn into life. She carried with her pollen from all three of the other trees, as well as empty vials for collecting. One of the local wise women who worked with the tree of rest was on old friend of Mary's. Her name was Seela, and she aided Mary in her work.

The task of labelling and cross-pollinating was done quietly and methodically. They divided the tree into three sections, one for the pollen of each of the three sisters and as the days passed Mary felt such a deep sense of peace growing inside her that she thought she could happily have stayed there for an age. Her time spent with the tree of rest was the complete antithesis of the time she had spent in the village of the tree of joy, yet both filled her heart with beauty and wonder and she would not have swapped either.

Seela knew the habits of the tree of rest well and Mary learned much from her. They talked about herbs and healing, and Mary told Seela of her resent adventures but mostly they worked in silence and absorbed the peaceful serenity of this place. Since the fruit of the tree of rest did not spoil as most fruit did they did not need to be harvested at a specific time. Also the fruit first became ripe in the winter and this was not a good time to travel. Mary was not young anymore and she had already travelled more this year then she had in the previous ten years. She was looking forward to the restfulness of winter.

They decided to leave the fruits on the tree until Mary returned for them the following year. Seela suggested that she would select three large healthy-looking fruits from each section of the tree and tie a golden ribbon around them so that nobody else would pick them before Mary came back. Then she promised that she would visit the tree regularly to check that all was well.

Mary thanked her kindly for her help with the work, for sharing her knowledge and her time with her, and for her hospitality and the healing softness of her company. She would like to have spent longer with the tree of rest because, in some ways it seemed most akin to her spirit, or perhaps it was just the ripeness of her years, but the winter would not wait and still her work was not over.

She headed south and east after she left Seela, back to the tree of love to collect the fruits of the flowers that she had pollinated there in the summer. The people of the village received her warmly, for they were indeed a warm people who lived near the tree of love, especially when it was in fruit. They told her that she could not fully understand the tree of love unless she had tasted its fruits but that this was not something to be done lightly. Furthermore, they explained to her that the consumption of this most sumptuous of fruits was such a significant occasion that the seeds were often treasured as a reminder of the event. Consequently, it could prove difficult to get anybody to part with them afterwards.

It was agreed that the best plan of action was for Mary to take some of the fruits home with her. There she would offer them as gifts to her close friends and family.

They could then enjoy the delights of the fruits of the tree of love and return the seeds to Mary so she could germinate them. In the end, she took six fruits, three from the crossing with the tree of wisdom and three from the tree of joy.

One of them she would share with her husband. Two she would give to her two closest friends and their partners, who were elders of her village. This left one for each of her three daughters and their husbands. The idea of returning home with these precious and magical gifts for her loved ones gave her great joy…

But when she reached her village she found that her home had even greater gifts waiting for her.

THE FOREST

One of the first things she did on arriving home was to go to the bottom of the garden and check the cold frames that housed the seeds she had planted at the end of the summer. These were the first seeds produced by crossing the trees of wisdom and of joy. As the children of the tree of joy each seed had been quite unique. They ranged from large wooden stones the size of mango or avocado seeds to handfuls of tiny grains smaller than sesame or poppy seeds. And now, only three months latter, she had in front of her an array of young seedling trees all as different as the seeds from which they sprouted.

The vibrancy and life of the new plants overwhelmed her. Already, the first few sets of leaves displayed every shade of green, form the lightest to the richest, as well as a selection of fine yellows and a scattering of whites and silvers. Some leaves were deeply veined or variegated, some had dark patches of red or even black, and one was covered in a thick layer of soft downy hairs that were nothing short of purple. Mary was overjoyed by the success of her first attempt at crossing the magical trees. She was also a little daunted by the volume of work she had taken on. To tend for so many trees of such different natures was a difficult enough task when one knew and understood them but she had first to figure out what each tree required.

This would be done partly by a process of deduction. She would infer their needs from their anatomy using what she had learned about plants from her travels and bearing in mind the habits of their parent trees. Part of the process would have to be trail and error; she would expose her new children to a variety of conditions and check their responses. But she had a sneaking suspicion that most of her decisions would come from something halfway between intuition and guesswork.

The fruits from the tree of love were presented to her friends and family and, when each was consumed, the seeds were returned to Mary. It is not part of this story to tell the tales of what happened to those friends and family members when they eat those exotic and provocative fruits except to say that for each it was an event that they did not forget for a long time.

Mary planted the seeds in neatly labelled pots, placed them in the cold frame and set about the process of a long and well-earned winter's rest. She knew well though that half of this rest would be spent remembering and dreaming about the trees and the adventures of that extraordinarily event-filled year and the other half would be spent imagining and planning for the adventures and the trees that might follow in the next.

Of coarse the winter was not entirely a time of rest because she now had three pollens to give to the tree of wisdom when it came into flower but this she did not consider work. In part because she did not have to journey away from her home to do it but mostly because the tree of wisdom was an old friend to her. It was her habit and her joy to visit it whenever time and the whether allowed so carrying some pollen with her was no great chore. Also she felt that the tree had given her so much, both in initiating the events of the previous year and in so many other ways throughout her life, that it was a pleasure to her to be able to pay it back in some way.

An early spring the next year brought fresh life and energy to the land and to all the plants and creatures that are part of her; including the people of the village of the tree of wisdom. Over the winter Mary had made careful plans of how she would go about the task of collecting and cross-pollinating the next generation of magical trees. But before she had even left her own village it became clear to her that mother nature had her own plans for the trees and they were not open for negotiation. It happened like this…

At the first signs of warmth, when the tree of wisdom was still in berry, the seeds from the tree of love that she had potted up in the fall began to germinate. Before long, the six seeds produced six small, similar looking seedlings. Similar they were, but not the same by any standard, and if differences could be discerned in such young plants, you could bet that the trees they produced would be noticeably different.

To most people this would have been an insignificant detail, if noticed at all, but not to Mary. She had expected the three seeds produced by crossing the trees of wisdom and love to produce identical plants, and the three seeds from the trees of joy and love to produce plants that were different from them but identical to each other.

You see she had assumed that when two trees were crossed a hybrid would be produced which was somewhere in the middle, probably half way, and that each time this process was repeated the same hybrid would result. She had been astonished and amazed by the great variety of plants born of the cross between the trees of wisdom and joy, but she assumed that this was due to the unusual fruiting habit of the latter.

When the seeds of the tree of love were given to her one by one the previous autumn, her keen eye had noticed subtle differences. But each was potted before the next arrived so it was difficult to compare them directly. She had also been weary from a year of traveling, so she had let the observation pass her by. Only now in the clear light of spring did she appreciate its significance.

She had thought that by crossing all four of the magical trees with each other she would produce a second generation of six hybrids. When this second generation were old enough to flower she would cross all six hybrids with each other and the four parent trees to produce forty-five new trees. She had fully accepted that by the third or fourth generation the number of possible combinations would become so large that it would take a small battalion of people to continue her work. Perhaps part of her had hoped that by that time her work would have inspired so many people that she might in fact have a battalion of helpers.

Perhaps it was just the thought that there was some degree of predictability in her work which had given her the energy to continue it so tirelessly and methodically.

The first crop of plants from the tree of joy had erupted a large molehill in her neatly mown mental lawn and she had spent much of the winter devising ways to trim around it. But now these more subtle differences in the offspring of the tree of love had shattered any hope of orderliness that she could cling to.

It was obvious to her now that any hybrid produced from crossing two trees would be a unique individual, just as any child of two parents is. It is probable that a second child of the same two parents would inherit characteristics of both those people, but very unlikely that they would appear in exactly the same quantity and proportions as those of their sibling. The same would also seem to be true of the magical trees; each seedling that sprouted was as unique and unpredictable a creation as the four magical trees from which they came.

Although this realisation ruined all her neatly made plans, once she had accepted it she felt a strange sense of freedom. It was as though she had been carrying around the idea that she was doing something of importance and, being a respectable old lady, she would do it well and properly; perhaps even scientifically but certainly to the best of her ability. Now she realised that she was merely a helper in the game of random creativity that was life.

Though her role was no less important she now saw that the trees were doing the work or rather that nature was working through the trees and it was a blessing for her just to be involved.

Mary prepared for her journey that year with new eyes. The pollen and seeds that she would carry, though no less carefully packed and neatly labelled, would no longer be numbers in her equation or sections in her plan. Now she would see each as divine gifts from the goddess; unique and precious offerings to the universe. The young trees in her care grew strong and healthy and, though she could see recognisable characteristics in them, she tried not to think of them in terms of their parents. She learned to view each tree as a newly awakened personality and got to know them as individual being. She named them and spoke to them as one might speak to a new-born baby or infant, not as one would speak to an ear of corn dancing idly in a field of ten thousand twins.

So she went out into the world again as full of enthusiasm and excitement as ever but with a deepened sense of mystery and wonder about the work that she was now only helping with. To begin with her task was much the same as it had been the previous year, the only difference being that she began with three sets of pollen for the already over productive tree of joy instead of one. Until the young trees at home began to flower, she still only had the four trees of Ebb's daughters to work with but she knew now the value of this work. She would not be repeating any of the previous year's works as she had once assumed.

It was not till late in the summer, when she had finally crossed every tree with every other tree, that things really began to change. For now, the young trees at home were large enough to plant out. In many ways this was the real beginning of her work. However many trees she bred personally, her time here was limited and it would all be for nothing if the process ended when she left. From the beginning her plan had been to plant out so many trees that she filled in all the gaps between Ebb's daughters, so that they were close enough to cross-pollinate each other.

She had given much thought over the previous year and a half as to how this might be done. Now she realised that the best technique would be an experienced, informed and loving randomness. On all her journeys so far, she had felt it somehow unlucky to walk in a straight line from one of the magical trees to another and so had always travelled in a graceful arc. Thus, she had described a great circle around the site of the original apple tree with which this story began.

She decided that she would begin planting out the young trees in this circle until all of Ebb's daughters were connected by a living chain of their progeny. Then she could begin to fill the circle in towards the centre until she reached the spot where Sky had cried Meadow into the world beyond. But for this, she would need help. She was happy to walk the countryside carrying vials of pollen and even small sacks of seed if necessary but she could not carry whole trees in pots and shovels.

Fortunately, there was no shortage of help. From her daughters and sons in law and grand children, to friends and other relatives, to people she had met on her travels, to complete strangers. It seemed that whenever she needed help, it was there and whenever she asked for help it was given willingly and joyfully. So, as the summer began to cool and the fresh autumnal winds tossed her hair and invigorated her senses, Mary set out from her home towards the tree of rest.

She took for the tree fresh pollen from her three sister trees and hoped to collect from it the seeds that Seela had selected the previous winter but for the first time she did not set out alone. She also had with her a cart-load of young trees and planting tools, as well as a small caravan of helpers and their possessions. The going was slower and less peaceful than she was used to and sometimes she was not sure whether she was an ageing gardener or a member of a noisy traveling circus group, or perhaps one of its attractions. But her heart was giddy with anticipation and her spirit danced at the thought of planting out the new trees.

The air was light and high that fall. Of the many memories Mary held from that journey sweetest of all was the joy of traveling with children and sharing with them the wonder of their first expedition away from home. Through their eyes she saw things anew and with their senses she heightened her perceptions. She spent a lot of time in the company of the children and learned much from their openness and honesty. Often she would ask their advice if she was unsure of something before she would ask the elders and just as often she was amazed by the directness and simple wisdom of their answers.

There were some places on the way that she knew to be special spots; suitable for special trees and she had only to choose the right tree to plant there. There were also some trees which she felt a special affinity towards. As if she knew them and their needs well and she simply had to wait for the right spot to manifest. Some plantings were spontaneous, impulsive, illogical or even almost accidental but there was an underlying sense of rightness about the entire journey. It was as if they were being gently guided. All they had to do was to listen carefully enough to the language of the land and of their own movements across it and nothing could go wrong.

So the year wound on. They sang and planted and chatted and planted their way to the village by the sea where the tree of rest faced west to the sunset and bathed peacefully in its amber glow. They stayed there for a week of so while Mary and Seela pollinated the tree and harvested last year's fruits and caught up on news and gossip. The other adults busied themselves with restocking the caravan's food supplies and catching up with old friend while the children delighted in making new friends and discovering new games to play and places to visit.

Then they were off again. South and east now to the tree of love to collect this year's fruit and to plant the remainder of their young trees on the way. Then, in what seemed like no time at all, the whirlwind subsided and the dreamlike hustle and bustle of activity ebbed its way back home.

Mary was glad to be back in her own house. She now had so many young plants in her garden that there was scarcely room to walk. The seeds from the tree of wisdom, which had sprouted out in the summer were getting quite large now and all needed to be repotted.

She placed the seeds that they had just collected from the tree of love into large clay pot and put them in the cold frame.

This year there had been no difficulty finding couples to eat the fruit of the tree of love. The members of her mobile arboretum had seen through a fair few of them before they ever reached home. While back at home the stories of what had happened to the people who eat them the previous year had been growing in the minds of her fellow villages and consequently there was a small queue of eager volunteers.

The trees that had grown out of the seeds of the tree of love from the previous year were now quite large and would be ready to be planted out in the spring. And every other space, pot and bucket in her garden was occupied by some bizarre and interesting young sprout from the abundant second crop of seeds from the tree of joy.

The fruit from the tree of rest she had harvested in a different manner than usual. Instead of twisting the fruit to reveal the wooden milk-filled cup, she had pulled from the stalk, thus removing the whole fruit. The round course hair covered globe seemed to snap off quite naturally here, at the point where Seela had tied the golden ribbons.

Maybe the tree had inferred from this gesture that these fruit were for sprouting and not for drinking.? Mary decided that she would germinate them indoors during the winter. She was growing accustomed to trusting these seemingly unfounded instincts and the fine healthy thick sprouts that emerged from these unlikely looking seeds at Christmastime proved her right again.

Whenever Mary had free time through the winter she visited the tree of wisdom up on the hill. Here she found peace and space for thought. She needed to think of ways to involve others more in her work. Already it was more than she could manage alone. One suggestion that occurred to her, or was given to her, quite early on was to find somebody in each of the four villages who could take on the job of germinating the seeds from their tree and then caring for the offspring until they were big enough to be planted out. She already had Seela in the village of the tree of rest and she had others in mind for the other trees. She was realising that the more people she involved in this work the more likely it was to succeed in the long term.

The next year a similar ramshackle caravan of people, plants and playing children accompanied Mary throughout her amblings and wanderings. As this impromptu train travelled, it grew. Slowly at fist but steadily and the stories and songs of its journeying grew too; until it was something of a legend in its own time. At the height of summer it was as if the whole of the mayday celebrations from the village of joy had decided to get up and go walkabout all together.

For Mary it was a time of shear delight. To be surrounded by so much joy and love and youthful exuberance in the twilight of her years was a blessing beyond compare. She drank in the days like a sweet honeydew nectar and, when the fires and the tale telling had died down, leaving only the stars to sing her to sleep, she dreamed of friendship and peace.

In the village of the tree of joy Mary stayed at her cousin's house as usual. She mentioned to her the idea of setting up a place in each of the four villages to raise the offspring of their trees. Her cousin was delighted by the suggestion and offered her services and her garden immediately. Then she took the idea several stages further. It seemed to be the nature of the people of that village that they considered a good idea to be wasted unless it was made as large and flamboyant as it could be and involved as many people as possible.

Mary's cousin decided that she would not only use her garden as a nursery for the young trees but she would turn her house into a school were the local children could learn all about the trees. She would teach them how to propagate and raise the trees and how and where to plant them out when the time came. She could teach them about pollination and crossbreeding as well as all manner of related botanical topics; from food production and general gardening, to knowledge of local flora. They could go out collecting herbs from the meadows and mushrooms and nuts and berries from the woodland. They could paint local trees and learn the magical and medicinal properties of them as well as their folklore.

So the ideas flowed. Mary was accustomed to the vivacious enthusiasm of the these people but when her cousin began to plan tree adoption schemes around the village for the time when her garden became too small, well she was quite astounded. Her normal steady minded reaction would have been to stop her cousin in her tracks and encourage her to be more practical and in the moment but she was enjoying letting go of the trees. She must let this process take its own life now; like a fledgling bird or a child leaving home, she must release it to its own destiny. So she smiled benevolently at her cousin and delighted in the unpredictability of it all.

The caravan moved more slowly than Mary had done when she was alone. Apart from the extra labour of tree planting, everything just seemed to take longer with larger number of people, larger meals to cook, camps to set up, children to look after, the list was endless. Mary revelled in the distraction now. They were the stuff of life and she loved it all.

Besides, since she was setting up the new planting stations in each village there was no need for them to double back to collect fruit as she had done, or to rush home eagerly to plant the seeds. Everything was done en route now. So the caravan just moved on one long slow circular journey that year following the seasons from one flowering magical tree to the next.

In the village of the tree of love there was a young couple who had met through the tree, fallen deeply in love and recently married. They were great fans of this botanical matchmaker and had helped Mary in her work the previous year. They offered to take over the job of collecting seeds from as many of the local people as they could get to part with them and of growing them on into young tress ready for planting. They helped again with this year's pollination while Mary gave them detailed instructions for the rest of their work. She told them that the caravan would return the following summer to collect the young trees, which it would "return to the wild" as it wandered its way through the rolling countryside.

They reached Seela's village a few days before the winds changed and Mary was glad to be under a roof again before this happened. Her spirits had been kept high by the joy of her vocation and by the energy of the life that surrounded her but she knew that almost three years now of traveling and sleeping under the stars was beginning to take its toll on her quietly ageing body. She was happy to be with Seela and the tree of rest. Seela already knew all that was needed and she convinced Mary to let her take charge immediately.

Initially Mary told herself that it would be a useful exercise to step back and see how smoothly the process ran without her. After a few days, when it was apparent that everybody was more than competent and all was going well, she began to really let them get on with it and spent more time walking alone and visiting the tree of rest. During their second week there the sea wind subsided and the still air warmed. Under Seela's guidance and watchful experienced eye Mary drank the milk from one of the fruit of the trees of rest. Seela had made her a nest of blankets and pillows under the tree and Mary curled up there and slept for three days.

When she woke she was frail and a bit giddy from the fast but she was bright eyed and shining. As well as feeling rested, she had also received inspiration about how to continue her work over the next few years as it got bigger and more complicated. She thanked the tree and she thanked Seela and two days latter they were off again but this time they were headed home.

Mary felt greatly refreshed on that journey. After her sleep under the tree of rest her energy was renewed. But she was still more than happy to except when her youngest daughter offered to help her in her garden with all the plants that remained. Apart from the trees she had brought home last year she had only to care for the children of the tree of wisdom now from her garden. Her youngest daughter also loved this tree and was keen to learn all her mother could teach her, to share in all her mother had learned over her recent journeys and to look after the work of rearing the offspring of the tree of wisdom in her mothers absence.

It was a comfort to Mary to have her daughter working so closely with her. They talked as they worked till they had put the world to rights and when all the words were spoken, they worked in silence simply enjoying the closeness of kin. It seemed appropriate to Mary that the care of the tree of wisdom should remain with her daughter and thus somebody who was also of Issy's bloodline.

It was also a relief to know that all four of the trees now had reliable guardians. This left Mary free for the work that was to come. Also, with her daughter taking charge of the tree of wisdom, she knew that after she had left this place and even after her task was long completed, her favourite of the four special trees would be well tended.

As well as finding trusted helpers to take over the growing of the next generation of magical trees, Mary had also been keen to find somebody who could lead the caravan on its annual migration and somebody who could supervise the plantings. In truth, this rather happened of its own accord and she had merely accepted and approved. From the first journey where help was needed her eldest daughter and son in law had been at her side.

He was strong and skilled with the ways of the road but more importantly, he was gentle and good with people. He was easy to talk to and slow to lose his temper. He could often see quickly to the bottom of problems or setbacks and found it easy to give instructions. Yet, he had such a kindness about him that it was a joy to do his bidding. Without appointment or argument he had naturally taken the role of leading the caravan. His advice was eagerly sought in confusion and his word was usually decisive in moments of confrontation or doubt.

When it came to the job of planting trees out into the landscape Mary's eldest daughter had always been there with her. She shared Mary's passion and enthusiasm for this work and she also shared her skill. In fact, it was possible that in this field she even surpassed her mother. Mary had always possessed an instinctive knowledge of the needs and dislikes of trees and an understanding of the land and the landscape which grew out of her deep connection to it. These were the skills she used to find suitable homes for her arboreal children.

But to her eldest daughter this process was something of an art form. She could perceive subtle energies in the land that Mary only noticed when hey were pointed out and she placed trees as if she were painting a landscape. She had an uncanny sense of how a tree would grow in a particular place and how the place and the tree would then grow into and around each other. Mary was more than happy to leave her precious babies in her daughter's safe hands.

THE HUNT

Early the next spring, when the people of the village of the tree of wisdom were beginning to stir from their cosy winter burrows and greet the rising air with bright-eyed yawning smiles, Mary set out. She set out alone again; long before the caravan was assembled and stocked and she set out in the opposite direction. She had been thinking about the first trees that were planted out. They were the offspring of the trees of wisdom, which flowered in the winter, and the tree of joy, which flowered in the spring. She guessed that the hybrids would flower somewhere in between the two parents and, since they were now over two years old, she wanted to see if she was right.

As usual, she was right, but not entirely. Many of the young trees were either in flower or about to flower. Some showed no signs of flowers, or even buds and, judging by the leaf litter underneath the trees, some she had clearly missed altogether. She marked each spot and remembered each tree with the accuracy of a hibernating animal storing seeds for the winter. From those trees that she managed to catch in flower, she took samples of pollen which she paid for with dustings of all the other pollens that she carried.

It was no longer feasible to label each bloom according to how it was pollinated in the hope of knowing the family history of the resultant plants. But the remnant of order still clung to Mary, so she devised a simple system that might help her to keep some track of the genetic lineage of the seeds she collected. She carried with her a bag containing rows of small glass vials. So far only four of these contained pollen, that of each the trees of Ebb's daughters. These were placed in seasonal order from winter through spring and round to autumn.

As she collected pollen from these newly flowering youngsters, she placed them in her bag in between the trees of wisdom and rest, in the direction in which she was walking. When she was pollinating a tree in the open countryside she started at the north face of the tree with pollen from the tree of wisdom and worked her way round by season, direction and tree. In this way, she hoped that when the fruits were collected she would know that those taken from the east side of any tree would be the children of that tree and the tree of joy.

She knew that even this much thoroughness would have to be abandoned before long but she felt that in these early stages it was good to keep as close a track of things as possible. This way she could ensure that every trees pollen was spread, that the most possible combinations of trees were tried and that if there was a problem with any of the trees she would be able to identify it easily and pay that tree more attention.

Even within this first group of trees, who shared the same two parents, the differences were already apparent. Some were clearly evergreen, with broad shiny deep green leaves. Some were clearly deciduous, with fresh new leaves just opening, or recently opened, or with large leaf buds ready to burst into life. A couple she was not quite sure whether the leaves had opened very early or had been there since the previous year and one or two as yet showed no signs of life all.

Some of the trees were squat, with the rounded modest posture of the tree of wisdom. Others were already quite sizeable and definitely reaching for the heavens like their fun loving easterly parent. And the flowers that she saw ranged from the unobtrusive delicate green/white humility of the tree of wisdom to the gaudy extravagance of the happiest tree in the land.

It was a delight to Mary to see her dreams coming to life and growing strong but she worked quickly and moved on because the year was still not fully warmed and she was keen to reach Seela's house. She ended up staying with Seela for most of that year. She journeyed southwards to check the trees that the caravan had planted on its way to the tree of love on its maiden voyage and then she returned to the village of the tree of rest.

Over the remainder of the spring and the summer she made a number of excursions into the countryside to check on the trees that had not flowered by her first visit, and to collect samples of fruits and seeds from those she had pollinated. But she also spent a lot of time visiting the tree of rest and helping Seela with her work. Mary learned much about the uses of herbs and trees in healing from Seela and together they tended the ever-increasing stock of young trees that were Seela's charge.

By late that summer she had seen most of this first generation of trees flowering and some of those that she had missed she had at least been able to identify their flowering time. You could be sure she would not miss them again next year. Some showed no sign of flowering at all and these she assumed would be the winter loving trees.

Others were just showing the first signs of flower buds when last she visited them. She marvelled that the offspring of a winter-flowering tree and a spring-flowering tree should choose to open its blossoms in the early autumn. She was slowly getting used to the fact that the only certain thing about working with nature was that it never behaved quite as one expected it to.

It was a quiet year for Mary. She enjoyed the peace and freedom of being out alone once more. Even when she was back in the village with Seela they often worked in silence. Mary found that she could listen to the land and the trees more carefully when she worked and walked by herself and this allowed her to fine tune her senses to the individual characters of the trees she encountered. When the caravan arrived in the village of the tree of rest in the early autumn it was like a firework carnival exploding noises and colours into their peaceful serenity.

The change was refreshing though and Mary was keen to know what had been happening in the other villages and to hear the news and the stories of the traveling gardeners. As well as bringing many new trees into the world, the caravan had also seen the birth of three babies that year, a fine fair-skinned boy and two darling dark-haired twin girls. The river of tales and enthusiasm was unstoppable and Mary had no desire to resist. She bade warm and grateful farewells to Seela and her friends from this seaside haven of tranquillity then, like a raft pushed out into a spring swollen mountain river, she allowed the ebullience of the caravan to carry her home.

Early the next spring Mary set out by herself again. This time however it was not for a restful summer gardening with Seela but to go in search of new flowers wherever that search might take her. By now she knew that the tress all around the circle of the caravan route would be mature enough to be flowering. She knew the where abouts and had a good idea of the habits of the trees she had visited last year (and planted the year before) but of the other others she had only the descriptions of the trees and their places provided for her by her eldest daughter. However detailed and accurate these were, they gave no guarantee to Mary that she would actually find them.

Mary had to back track many times in order to catch as many trees in flower as possible. Sometimes she felt as though she was walking round in circles. She spent a short amount of time based at Seela's house but by late that spring she was in the village of the tree of love. She spent some time there helping and advising her two young friends who were rearing the seeds of this tree. She left with them samples of all the pollen she had collected from the new trees to offer to the tree of love when it came into flower. She thanked them and blessed them for their help and then she was off.

Now her senses were sharp for she was seeking out trees that she had only seen before as young seedlings in pots. Some of the places her daughter had described were places she knew well and these trees would be relatively easy to find. But it is the nature of life on a caravan that many things happen haphazardly and some of the directions she had were at best vague. If Mary had any defining characteristics however it was determination and now this shone forth.

Wherever she walked she scanned the countryside with the eyes of a hovering hawk; hungry and sharply awake. Any sign of a distant tree that looked slightly different to its neighbours or a feature in the land that resembled one of her daughter descriptions and her nostrils flared. Like a bloodhound on the trail of an injured quarry, she followed every lead relentlessly.

Some time in the early summer, half way between the villages of the trees of love and joy, Mary met up with the caravan traveling in the opposite direction. She camped with them for three nights exchanging news and enjoying the homeliness of conversation and a shared fire. The caravan was now wandering deeper into the circle in search of suitable places for planting out their precious charge.

Mary encouraged them in this. She felt it was time for the band of magical trees to grow thicker and begin to fill in the circle. She also instructed her daughter to encourage anybody who showed an interest in their work to become involved for soon they would need places in many more than four villages to help them to propagate the trees. Then, refreshed from the exchange of ideas, she set off again.

She reached the village of the tree of joy late in the day on the eve of mid summer. A pulsating amber orb of sunlight sank lazily into the western horizon as she crested the last hill while a plump ochre moon rose full and fecund in the east and all across the land a choir of red and yellow bonfires danced bright melodies over this stately celestial chord of colour. The air was alive with excitement and possibility and Mary felt that even if she had she been transported her blindfold she would have recognised this place as the village of the tree of joy from the happy tingling of her flesh.

At her cousins house she was greeted with a vibrant chorus of welcomes as a skirtful of hugging children almost prevented her from getting through the door. Mid-summer's eve was a night of high festivity in the village; but then they were well known to have more festivals in the average month then most people celebrated in a round year. This fact gave Mary no source for complaint this evening though.

After a marvellous feast set against the screams and songs of playing children, who seemed to find no difficulty eating and continuing their games at the same time, everybody wrapped up in shawls and jackets, though the night was warm, and set off to find the bonfires. The village of joy was on top form. There was music everywhere, people dancing and entertaining each other with feats of magic and trickery. Jugglers and acrobats passed as frequently as butterflies in a summer meadow, people everywhere were dressed in fancy hats or costume dress and then, when Mary felt she had drunk her fill of colours and sounds, the fireworks began.

These were fireworks like she had never seen them. She had heard stories of the fireworks at the mid-summer festival in the village of joy but she had thought them to be over woven with imagination and excessive eloquence, as most stories are. This evening she felt that if anything they had been understated. Perhaps her senses were heightened, having spent so much of the year in solitude searching sharp-eyed for distant details, but to Mary that night the firework display was simply otherworldly.

From the first vibrant green shower of light she was transported into a quivering spire of delight. Then she was carried for the rest of the night on an enchanted journey of yellow and golden, blue and red, purple and pink, and brilliant white. Twisting and turning in rainbows of iridescent fancy she watched the stars in carnival wrapping round each other like the rushing knots of children. Or curtseying and bowing in some courtly arabesque danced by a thousand devas at the fearie queen's wedding.

By the end of the evening Mary felt as though her time spent walking in the open countryside in search of trees was a feint and distant memory, even though she had been fully immersed in it that very morning. The first light of the longest day of the year was lifting pale signs of blue back into the eastern sky when they finally returned to her cousin's house. Mary felt she could have slept for a month but sleep was the one luxury she was not allowed to indulge in. Sleep in the village of joy at mid-summer was time wasted; there was far too much celebrating to be done.

In fairness she did manage to sleep for a few hours until the sounds of the children's games and the smells of breakfast cooking became more enticing than her dreams. The festivities continued through the day. Some of them centred around the tree of joy and thus related to Mary's work but many did not and she did not care. For a moment she had resigned herself to the whirlwind that is life in the village of joy and she would ride this most pleasant of storms to its end.

In all Mary spent a month at her cousin's house that year. After the mid-summer festivities had passed she spent a lot of time helping her cousin with the school. As schools go it was an informal affair; people came and went as they pleased. Some had assumed particular responsibilities or chores, some had ongoing personal projects, some came just to help out or to pass the time of day. Most of the village children passed through at some point in the day, as well as a fair few adults. The atmosphere was light and playful but Mary and her cousin were subjected to a constant stream of questions or requests for assistance and there was a definite air of learning about the place.

Mary enjoyed sharing her knowledge. For knowledge is one of those special substances that you only realise how much you have when the time comes to share it and the more you give away the more you have left. There was also another reason why she chose to stay so long with these children. She hoped that here she might find one or two youngsters who showed that special interest in trees that she felt. Not a passing curiosity that any child might display for something new or well taught but a passion that ran deeper.

She was looking for protégés. Children whose eyes lighted at the sight of a seed sprouting into new life, children whose heart sang with the land when a young tree was planted out in that perfect spot, where it had somehow always belonged. And more than this she was looking for that edge of wildness of spirit; youngsters who were excited by the prospect of discovering new things and who were not afraid to go off alone or to stand alone if it were necessary.

Her status as visitor allowed her the luxury of favouritism and she displayed this shamelessly, lavishing large amounts of her attention on those special few who responded to her subtle tests. She wanted more than anything to make sure that their interest in and passion for this work flowered so that they might carry on her wandering when she was no longer able to do so.

You may remember also that every year the tree of joy produced a single apple. Well that summer, with great pomp and ceremony, it was presented to Mary; a very valid reason for an extra celebration. This act touched her deeply. She decided that if the seeds of this apple produced any new trees she would take them to the hill on the land that once belonged to Ebb and plant them there were the original apple tree had long lived.

Another point of note is that that year the tree of joy bore, on the same branch, two identical fruits. To the knowledge of the village people, this had never happened before. Mary thought that they might be twin fruits, perhaps a blessing from the tree to the twins born on the caravan the previous year. Each fruit contained one large stone. Mary gave instructions that these seeds should be very carefully labelled and raised and, when they were large enough, the young trees should be planted near to each other. This was just as well for it transpired that Mary was quite wrong. But this she did not learn for some years and will tale that tale when we reach it.

Before long the moon was waxing towards its peak again. As it began to dominate the night sky so the sun seemed to cower away from the day. Or else it was losing interest in its northern holiday. For it seemed to barely find the time to visit now on the way to its southern friends. One grey cloud covered day when the sun popped in for only the briefest of hellos and slammed the door with a gusty blow on its way out Mary decided it was time to head home.

Soon the whether would begin to pack up its summer clothes and Mary had work yet to complete before she could lay down her tools for the winter. So she said her farewells and the day after the full moon she set out early to a chorus of busy birds under a crisp clear sky towards her home and a well-earned winters rest.

The next year Mary began her wanderings before the last of the snow had melted. Now they were real wanderings. There were so many trees already planted out that there was no way she could cover them all. She offered up the last vestiges of order and placed all her trust in good lady luck, the winds of fortune and, not least of all, her well trained nose.

So sharp was her ability to find these small flowering shrubs in this expansive half-tamed landscape that it appeared uncanny to others. It was as though she could feel their presence before sight or smell had a chance to speak. Once she knew that a plant was near nothing could shake her from the trail until it was discovered. So dogged was her determination that she became known as Mary the flower Hunter.

Her determination was matched only by her memory for she held in her mind every detail of every plant she had visited. Its position, its size and manner, its time of flowering and fruiting, the shape, colour and size of its leaves, all were stored in her thoughts as clearly as if she kept a dairy with photographs. She could also give wonderfully accurate descriptions of all the flowers she had seen and scents she had smelt and, for many if not most trees, she knew their lineage. Even where she had not seen a tree planted she could usually guess just by looking at it which two parents it came from.

The caravan travelled further afield again in search of good spots to plant out their charges. All the trees they passed from previous years seemed to be growing well and strong but then the caravan itself was also growing well and strong. In fact, quite without anybody noticing it had almost doubled in size and was being added to almost daily.

Wherever there is a sizeable gathering of people there will be traders ready to ply their wares. From the necessities of food and clothing to the frivolities of ornament and fancy somebody would have something to fit the bill. From dairymaids to jewellers, from fruit farmers to fortune-tellers, the caravan became a mobile Mecca for all manner of merchants. With every village that it passed through a small crowd would leave with them. Most would drift back to their homes after a day or twos holiday but some remained with the caravan for the rest of the year.

The next year and the caravan continued to grow and Mary continued in her wanderings. Now they were almost completely without direction for the entire circle of the four villages of Ebb's daughters was becoming filled with the flowers of their progeny. The caravan's journey was more of a cross than a circle now as it tried to find spaces for the new trees. It headed south out of the village of the tree of wisdom and meandered its way towards Ebb's valley. Before it reached there it had planted all the trees it carried and it turned east towards the village of joy for fresh supplies

Late that summer after a visit to the village of the tree of love the caravan had arranged to meet with Mary on the farm where Ebb once lived. Together there they planted one of the young trees that had grown from the apple of the tree of joy. They stayed there for three days and nights. One of these nights Mary spent alone on the hill where the new young apple tree was planted and in her thoughts she spoke to Ebb and to Sky and Meadow.

She told them some of the many wonderful stories that laced the lives of the trees they had nurtured. She told them how much they had helped and served and inspired the peoples of these lands for so many generations. Above all she thanked them for being part of a venture that had contributed so much to her life and the lives of many others, known and unknown. In the last part of the night she drifted into a deep magical sleep where she dreamed of stars and flowers and gods and the Mother. She woke at the first light of a clear summer dawn and felt awake and alive, thoroughly refreshed and moved almost to tears at the beauty of the day and the wonder of the world.

After Mary left the caravan she had an urge to visit the two trees born from the twin fruits of the tree of joy. For years, these had been thought of as twins themselves. They had eventually been planted out by the caravan on opposite sides of a small stream not far from the village of love where they grew strong and tall and were cared for fondly by the folk of that village.

When Mary arrived there that year they were just coming into flower for the first time and only now was the true nature of their relationship understood. They were in fact a male and a female form of the same tree. This was the first time the magical trees had produced such a couple and Mary was delighted, so too, as you can imagine, were the people from the village of love.

This would help with the ever-increasing variety of magical trees because they would cross very easily with each other and hopefully bare many varied children. It was probable that being such a close match and so closely planted that they would cross without aid and self-seed. Somehow these two trees also told Mary that the children of the four magical trees were becoming slowly more like the other trees of the earth and that one day soon they would be able to cross breed with them. To Mary this would be the beginning of the end of her work. Once she knew that the offspring of Ebb's daughters could interbreed with all the other trees that surrounded them she could be sure that the special qualities that they represented would be preserved for all time.

The following year Mary set out with the caravan. She hoped that by starting in the opposite direction to her normal travels she would find flowers that she had missed on previous years. Before long she left the caravan and went out on her own but not for months at a time as she used to. She decided it was good to have them near so she came back to them regularly like a dog being walked runs after rabbits and new smells but keeps the whereabouts of it walker in mind and circles back when the hunt is through.

By the end of that year the caravan had grown to the size small village. When it visited other villages for supplies now it set up camp just outside the villages rather than entering into them for fear that there would be no room left for the residents. Many of the other towns and villages around that area now had places devoted to the propagation of the new generations of magical trees so the caravan was no longer restricted in its route to the village where the trees of Ebb's daughter grew.

Its annual ramblings had become quite a local institution. It was thought of as half way between a travelling circus and a moving market town. The number and variety of its occupants had swelled so much that tree planting seemed little more than a minor sideline than its main purpose. Indeed a passing stranger could have been forgiven for not noting this as one of its activities at all.

Mary also developed something of a reputation. Tales of her wanderings were common fireside fodder and her name was often substituted into adventures that she had no part in. To the generation of children that followed, "Mary the Hunter" was a mythical character possessed of magical powers and credited with great feats. Though in truth her energy and insight were nothing short of miraculous and the achievements of herself and the people she inspired were great by any reckoning.

For thirteen years in all Mary roamed the countryside seeking out the trees that she called Ebb's grandchildren. Spreading pollen, collecting new seeds and hunting down rare and unusual hybrids filled her days and her thoughts but the adventures that she tumbled through on the way were many and varied. Since that night on Ebb's hill she dreamed often of heavenly landscapes inhabited by otherworldly beings of light and beauty; dreams from which she woke feeling deeply refreshed. Her vibrant nature and boundless enthusiasm were infectious and all those who encountered her were touched by her simple joy of life.

Towards the end of her travels she was regularly finding young self-seeded trees that were born of both the local worldly trees and Ebb's daughters, or granddaughters. Though, quite how she knew this nobody else was sure. To Mary it meant that the future of her precious tree of wisdom and her three sisters was ensured. So, at the request of common sense and her old bones she decided it was time to hang up her walking shoes not that she didn't intend to regularly take them down again for smaller outings- they do say old habits die hard.

Mary spent the last three years of her life rediscovering her home, playing with her grandchildren and writing her memoirs. At first, she intended these to be a practical botanical guide to the magical trees, their origin and their cultivation. But, like all her neatly laid plans, they soon became filled with so many other events relating to the planting of the trees and to her life that she soon reconciled herself to writing them in more autobiographical form. Though it should be said that later copies of what was titled " the Dairies of Mary the Hunter" read more like a book of fearie tales.

With time Mary began to hear the call of the land stronger than the call of any bed. For the weariness that comes at the end of a life does not compare with that of the end of any day. She shared her last songs with her grandchildren and blessed and caressed her loved ones then curled up at the foot of her favourite tree and was engulfed there in the folds of a dream so sweet that it would take her all of eternity to complete its dreaming.

But her work did not stop. When Mary left this place, not a small battalion, but a veritable army of helpers was beavering away, keeping her vision alive and not least of these were the birds, the insects and the wind. There were so many magical trees now that they were freely crossing with each other and with the other trees of the world and they were seeding themselves wherever the wind or their winged carriers would take them.

The land encompassed by the four trees planted by Ebb's daughters was a gold mine of unusual and beautiful flora and they were slowly beginning to spread out in every direction. Some say that all the trees that grow today are descended from these and that if you examine a modern tree with your eyes and your heart you will find in it one or more of the characteristics of Ebb's daughters. Wherever I have looked I have found this to be true but why not try it for yourself and see.

When you sit under a tree and breath in its essence does it fill your body with such a deep sense of peace that you leave feeling refreshed and healed? Or does it fill your spirit with such a joy of life that you dance away with a spring in your step and a song on your tongue? Does it perhaps help you to clear your mind so that you can see through to the source of any problem and, through understanding, find your way to forgiveness and compassion?

Or does it fill your heart with such a gentle and profound love that you become immersed in waves of fondness and affection which flow out to all your loved ones and then overflows to all their loved ones and still further to all their loved ones. And on and on until you have wrapped a warm blanket of love around all the beings and creatures and plants of the earth and the earth itself... and beyond?

If so, then you have spent a moment with one of the great great grandchildren of Ebb's daughters.

dedicated to my loving wife Alison

with special thanks
to my mum Anne for her endless giving
and Luisa Batista for encouragement and proof reading

and to all those known and unknown
with whom we all inter-are

Printed in Poland
by Amazon Fulfillment
Poland Sp. z o.o., Wrocław

15982432R00056